HELPING YOUR BRA

Here's how to make first-time reading easy and fun:

▶ Read the introduction at the beginning of each story aloud. Look through the pictures together so that your child can see what happens in the story before reading the words.

▶ Read one or two pages to your child, placing your finger under each word.

▶ Let your child touch the words and read the rest of the story. Give him or her time to figure out each new word.

▶ If your child gets stuck on a word, you might say, *"Try something. Look at the picture. What would make sense?"*

▶ If your child is still stuck, supply the right word. This will allow him or her to continue to read and enjoy the story. You might say, *"Could this word be 'ball'?"*

▶ Always praise your child. Praise what he or she reads correctly, and praise good tries too.

▶ Give your child lots of chances to read the story again and again. The more your child reads, the more confident he or she will become.

▶ Have fun!

Text copyright © 2007 by Christine Webster
Illustrations copyright © 2007 by Tim Nihoff

All rights reserved.

First edition 2007

Library of Congress Cataloging-in-Publication Data is available.

Library of Congress Catalog Card Number 2006049587

ISBN 978-0-7636-2921-2

2 4 6 8 10 9 7 5 3 1

Printed in China

This book was typeset in Letraset Arta.
The illustrations were created digitally.

Candlewick Press
2067 Massachusetts Avenue
Cambridge, Massachusetts 02140

visit us at www.candlewick.com

Otter Everywhere

CANDLEWICK PRESS
CAMBRIDGE, MASSACHUSETTS

Christine Webster
illustrated by Tim Nihoff

Contents

Otter's Picnic 1

Otter Makes Bubbles 11

Otter Goes Swimming 21

Otter's Apples 31

Otter's Picnic

Introduction

This story is called *Otter's Picnic*.
It's about how Otter goes on a picnic
but ants keep taking her food.
And then they take Otter!

Otter has a banana.

Otter has an apple.

Otter has cheese.

Ants take the banana.

Ants take the apple.

Ants take the cheese.

The ants take Otter!

Otter and the ants have a picnic.

Otter Makes Bubbles

Introduction

This story is called *Otter Makes Bubbles*. It's about how Otter makes so many bubbles in her bath, she gets hidden!

Otter is taking a bath.

She pours soap in the water.

The soap makes bubbles.

She pours more soap in the water.

The soap makes lots of bubbles.

Where is Otter?

Achoo! Otter sneezes.

There's Otter!

Otter Goes Swimming

Introduction

This story is called *Otter Goes Swimming*. It's about how Otter gets ready to swim in her pool. She puts on so many things that there's no room in the pool for her!

Otter puts on her swimsuit.

Otter fills the pool.

Otter puts on her swim cap.

Otter puts on her lifesaver.

Otter puts on her goggles.

Otter puts on her flippers.

Otter jumps into the pool.

There's no room for Otter!

Introduction

This story is called *Otter's Apples*. It's about how one apple falls and Otter picks it up. Another apple falls, and Otter picks it up. When *Otter* falls, *lots* of apples fall. Then Otter makes something special with all the apples!

An apple falls.

Otter picks it up.

Another apple falls.

Otter picks it up.

Otter falls.

ALL the apples fall.

Otter picks them up.

Otter makes apple pies.